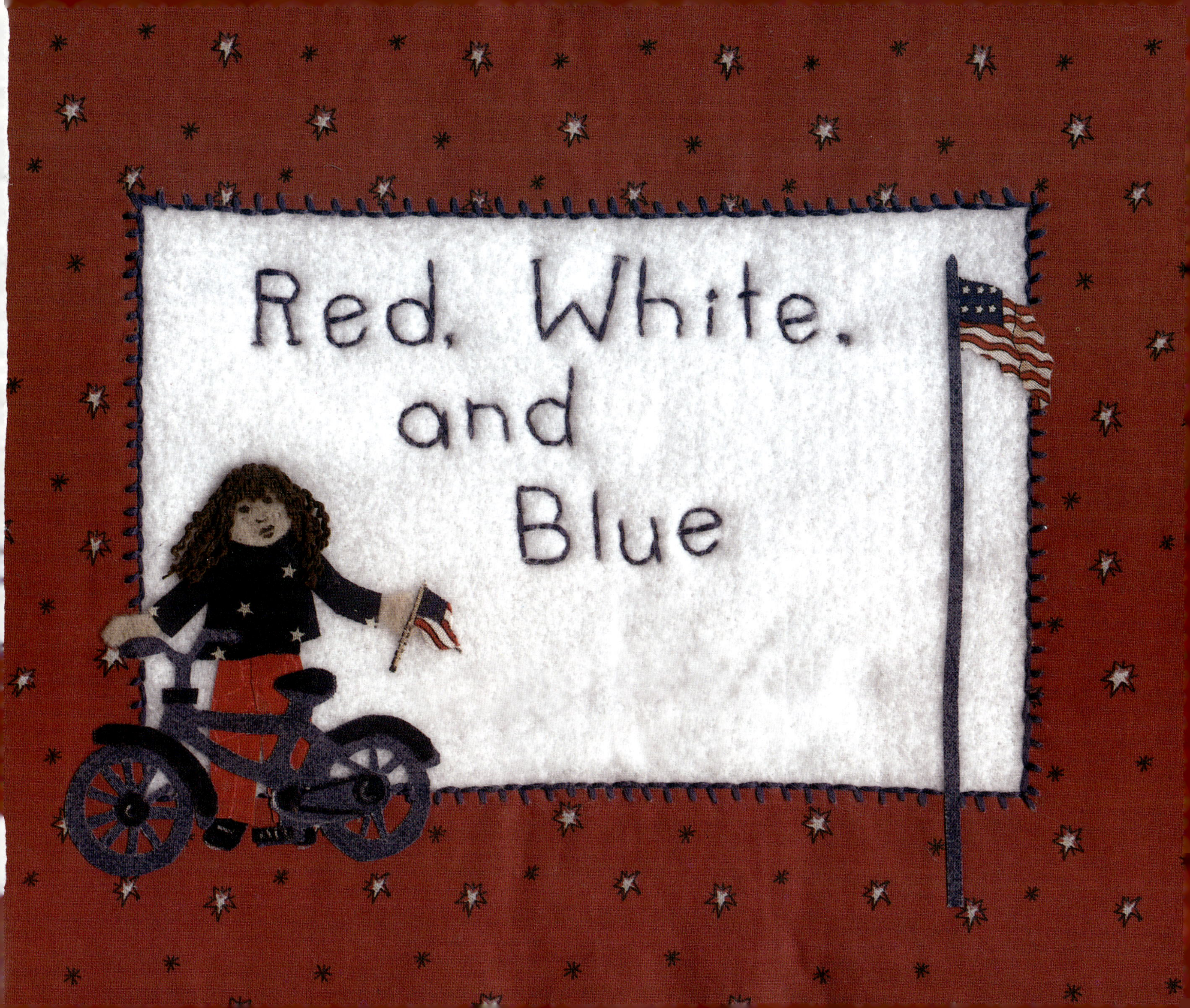
Red, White,
and
Blue

Red, White, and Blue

by
Laurie Lazzaro Knowlton

PELICAN PUBLISHING COMPANY
Gretna 2002

To all who devote their lives to serving the United States of America—
God bless you and yours

The word "Pelican" and the depiction of a pelican are trademarks
of Pelican Publishing Company, Inc., and are registered
in the U.S. Patent and Trademark Office.

Library of Congress Cataloging-in-Publication Data

Knowlton, Laurie Lazzaro.
  Red, white, and blue / Laurie Lazzaro Knowlton.
    p. cm.
  ISBN 1-58980-055-9 (pbk. : alk. paper) — ISBN 1-58980-067-2
(hardcover : alk. paper)
  1. Flags—United States—Juvenile poetry. 2. Liberty—Juvenile
poetry. 3. Children's poetry, American. 4. Patriotic poetry, American.
[1. Flags—Poetry. 2. Liberty—Poetry. 3. American poetry] I. Title.
  PS3561.N6835 R43 2002
  811'.54—dc21

                          2002006345

Printed in Korea

Published by Pelican Publishing Company, Inc.
1000 Burmaster Street, Gretna, Louisiana 70053

pointing to the heavens announcing, "One notion, under God!"

I see you, Red,
White, and Blue,
blowing in the
breeze,

one nation, under God,
liberty and justice for all.
for which it stands, one nation
indivisible with liberty and
to the flag of the

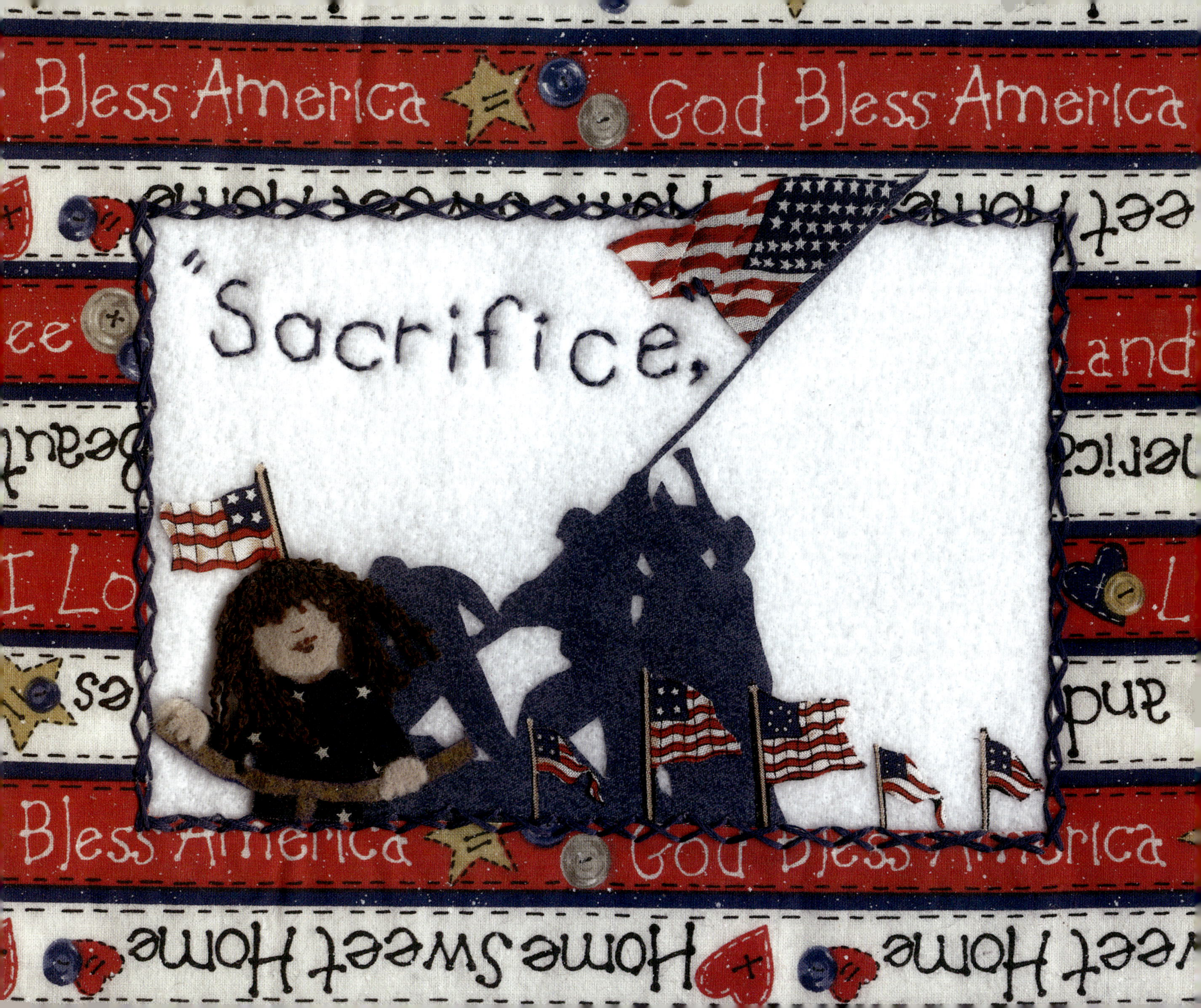
Bless America
God Bless America
"Sacrifice,
Home Sweet Home

"Loyalty,"

I pledge allegiance to the flag

of the United States of America

and to the republic for which it stands,

one nation, under God,

indivisible,

with liberty and justice for all.

Our people
may be of every
color,
but we are united
by the

From
North to South,
East to West.

your colors
SNAP

the flag of the United States of America and to the republic for which it stands, one nation, under G
d to the republic for which it stands, one nation, under God, indivisible, with liberty and justice for
of America and to the republic for which it stands, one nation, under God, indivisible, with liberty a
United States of America and to the republic for which it stands, one nation, under God, indivisible,
republic for which it stands, one nation, under God, indivisible, with liberty and justice for all. I pledge
giance to the one nation,
States of A ible, with lib
ica and to t y and justice
which it sta egiance t
ited States le, wi
America an erty and j
to the repub ice for all. I
the flag of t under Go
d to the rep ice for a
of America liberty an
United States divisible, wi
ublic for or all. I pledge
ance to the one nation, u
States of A le, with libe
ca and to ti justice f
hich it stan giance to
ted States of America and to the republic for which it stands, one nation, God, sible, with
America and to the republic for which it stands, one nation, under God, i le, erty and ju
the republic for which it stands, one nation, under God, indivisible, w rty and tice for all. I p
he flag of the United States of America and to the republic for which t ds, one nation, under God
to the republic for which it stands, one nation, under God, indivisible, with liberty and justice for all.

Freedom !

Freedom to Worship.

My flag answers to many names:

"Old Glory,"
"The Stars
and Stripes,"

But to me you
will forever be
my Red, White,
and Blue.